Weekly Reader Children's Book Club presents

# SMALL DEER'S MAGIC TRICKS

By Betty Boegehold

Drawn by Jacqueline Chwast

Coward, McCann & Geoghegan, Inc.     New York

ISBN 0-698-30659-7 (lib. bdg.)

This book is a presentation of Weekly
Reader Children's Book Club.
Weekly Reader Children's Book Club
offers book clubs for children from
preschool to young adulthood. All
quality hardcover books are selected
by a distinguished Weekly Reader
Selection Board.

For further information write to:
**Weekly Reader Children's Book Club**
1250 Fairwood Ave.
Columbus, Ohio 43216

*Printed in the United States of America*

# CONTENTS

## Small Deer's Magic Bag

Long ago
a small deer lived in faraway Borneo.
She was called Small Deer
because she was so small.
She was also very smart.

Tiger lived there, too.
He was always trying
to catch Small Deer.

One morning Tiger found some
golden grapes.

He said, "Small Deer likes grapes.

She will come here to eat them.

Then I will catch her."

Tiger hid behind a bush and waited.
Soon Small Deer came
trotting along, trippity-trip.
She was carrying a big brown bag
to fill with golden grapes.

"Aha!" shouted Tiger, jumping out.
"I've caught you at last, Small Deer!"

Small Deer's little legs trembled,
but she was thinking fast.
She said, "No, no, Tiger.
I can't let you catch me today.
I am on my way to the king.
I must do my magic trick for him."

"What magic trick?" asked Tiger.

"I can make two things
out of one thing," said Small Deer.
"I've been doing it all week.
Now the king wants me
to make two kings out of one king.
So I must hurry."

Tiger was thinking, too. He said,
"I will let you go, Small Deer.
But first you must make
two tigers out of one tiger."

"Very well," said Small Deer.

"First, you must jump
into my magic bag."

"Why?" asked Tiger.

"Because I do my magic trick with
my magic bag," Small Deer said.
"So hurry up and jump in."

Without another word
Tiger jumped into the bag.
Small Deer pulled the string tight.

Then, trippity-trip,
she went on through the woods.

Bump. Bang. Bangity-bump.
The bag bumped
over the sticks and stones.
"Ow! Ow!" cried Tiger.
"You are hurting me, Small Deer!"

"Be brave, Tiger," said Small Deer,
"for this is the way
to make two tigers out of one tiger.
Now I am almost done."

So saying, Small Deer
came to the riverbank. Splash!
Small Deer pushed the bag,
Tiger and all, into the river.
Down the river went the bag
turning round and around
with Tiger inside.

"Help! Help!" yelled Tiger.

"Small Deer has tricked me!"

Another tiger was walking
along the bank of the river.
When she heard Tiger yelling,
"Help! Help!"
the other tiger grabbed a stick,
pulled the bag ashore.
Tiger leaned against a tree.

"Small Deer tricked me!"
he roared.
"She said she would make
two tigers out of one tiger.
Then she pushed me in the river!
I will catch her and eat her up!"

"Wait," said
The Other Tiger.
She looked
at Tiger.
Then she looked at herself.
"But there *are* two tigers," she said.
"There are two tigers here now."

Tiger stopped roaring.
He looked at The Other Tiger.
Then he looked at himself.
He counted slowly, "One tiger
and one more tiger
makes two tigers!
Small Deer didn't trick me!
She made two tigers
out of one tiger after all!"

Then the two foolish tigers
ran off to tell the king.
But far away, under the trees,
Small Deer ate golden grapes
all afternoon.

## Fair's Fair

The Oldest-of-All-Crocodiles
was sleeping in the soft mud
on the bank of the river.

Crash! A tree fell over
right on top of Crocodile!
He couldn't even wiggle his tail.
"Help! Help!" shouted Crocodile.

Water Buffalo came by. She said,

"What is the matter, Crocodile?"

"Help! Help!" shouted Crocodile.
"The tree fell over on top of me!
I can't even wiggle my tail!"

"I will help you," said Water Buffalo.
She put her strong head
against the tree.

Shove. Push. Shove.

Soon the tree rolled over
and Crocodile was free.

Then, with a great crocodile smile,
the Oldest-of-All-Crocodiles
grabbed Water Buffalo by her leg.

"I'm hungry now," said Crocodile.
"You will make a good lunch for me."

Water Buffalo cried,
"But I just helped you!
You are not fair, Crocodile!"

Crocodile answered,
"Of course I'm fair.
I need lunch, so I must eat you."

"No, no!" said Water Buffalo.
"That's not fair, Crocodile.
Ask anyone if that's fair!"

"Very well," said Crocodile, still
holding on to Water Buffalo's leg.
"I will ask the first one
who passes by.
You will see that I am fair."

Soon Small Deer came along.

"Stop, Small Deer!"
cried Water Buffalo.
"Say that Crocodile isn't fair!
I rolled the tree off him,
and now he wants to eat me!"

"No, no, Small Deer,"
shouted Crocodile. "You must say
that I *am* fair!  I'm hungry
and I have caught Water Buffalo.
So it's fair to eat her for lunch."

Small Deer
sat down on the riverbank.

"Please stop shouting," she said.
"I can't think well if you shout.
And I must think. I must think
if Crocodile is fair or not fair."

Crocodile and Water Buffalo
stopped shouting.
They didn't say a word.
But Crocodile kept holding on to
Water Buffalo's leg.

Small Deer closed her eyes.
She asked herself,
"Is Crocodile fair? Or not fair?"

Then she opened her eyes and said,
"You both must show me
just what happened. Then I will know
if Crocodile is fair or not fair."

"That is a good idea,"
Water Buffalo said.

"Yes, yes, that's a very good idea,"
said Crocodile. "We will do it again.
We'll show Small Deer
just what happened!"

Crocodile let go
of Water Buffalo's leg.
And Water Buffalo
put her strong head down
against the fallen tree.

Push. Shove. Push, shove, push.
Water Buffalo rolled the fallen tree
back on top of Crocodile.

"That's just what happened,"
said Water Buffalo. "I found
Crocodile under the fallen tree."

"Yes, yes," said Crocodile.
"I was yelling for help, like this:
Help! Help!"

"Then I pushed the tree away
and he was free," said Water Buffalo.
She put her head down
to push the tree.

Small Deer sprang to her feet.
"Wait, wait!" she called.
"I know the answer now!  I know
whether Crocodile is fair or not fair."

"Tell us at once," cried Crocodile
and Water Buffalo together.

Small Deer looked at Water Buffalo.
"It's fair for Crocodile
to want some lunch
when he is hungry," said Small Deer.

Then she looked at Crocodile.
"But it is *not* fair," she said,
"for you to eat Water Buffalo
after she has freed you.
So you are fair and *not* fair, Crocodile."

Small Deer
looked again at Water Buffalo.
"And it's fair for Water Buffalo
to run away very fast when
someone wants to eat her for lunch."

Water Buffalo smiled.
"Yes," she said. "Fair's fair.
Good-bye, Crocodile."
And away ran Water Buffalo
holding her strong head high.

On the riverbank
Small Deer looked at Crocodile
under the fallen tree.
"Ask me anytime," she said.
"I'll always be glad to tell you
when you are fair
or not fair."

But the Oldest-of-All-Crocodiles
only said, "Help! Help!"

# War on Small Deer!

Many crocodiles lived in a river
near Small Deer's home.
The crocodiles would not let her
cross the muddy river.
"Go the long way around,"
they would shout.
"No one can cross our river!"

One day, Small Deer wanted to play
in the field of green reeds
on the other side of the river.
"If I go the long way around,"
she said to herself,
"the sun will be going down.
So I will think of a way
to cross the river."

The crocodiles
clashed their terrible teeth
and lashed the water
with their terrible tails.

"Go away, Small Deer!"
they shouted all together.
"You cannot cross our river!"

"Listen to me, crocodiles,"
called Small Deer.
"The king has sent me
to count all the animals.
The animals
who have the biggest number
will win a prize.

I have counted
the pigs and elephants.
Now I will count you."

The crocodiles stopped clashing
their terrible teeth and lashing
the water with their terrible tails.
The Oldest-of-All-Crocodiles said,
"Count us, Small Deer,
for surely we will win the prize."

"Very well," answered Small Deer.
"Line up, all of you,
so I can count you one by one."

The crocodiles lined up, one by one,
all across the muddy river.
Only their big eyes and noses
stuck out of the water.

Small Deer jumped
onto the nose of the first crocodile.
"One crocodile," said Small Deer.
Then she jumped onto the nose
of the second crocodile.
"Two crocodiles," she said.
"Stay very still, all of you."

All the crocodiles stayed very still.
They didn't clash their terrible teeth
or lash their terrible tails.
Small Deer jumped
from nose to nose.
She kept counting and counting.

"Three, four, five," said Small Deer.

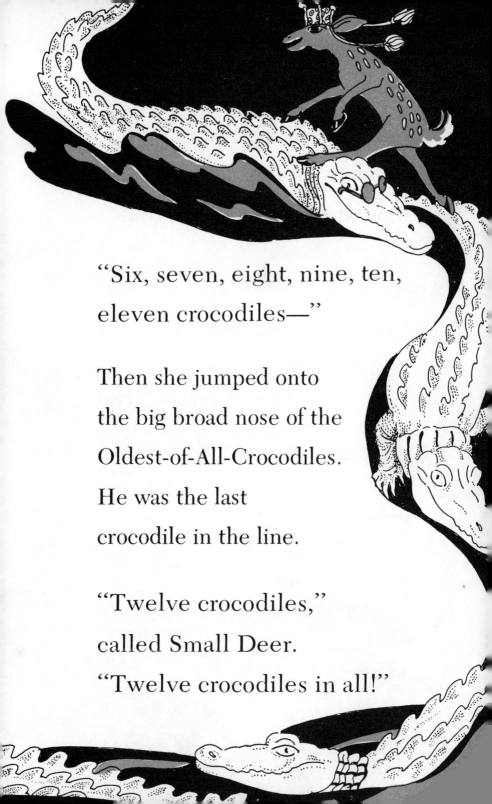

"Six, seven, eight, nine, ten,
eleven crocodiles—"

Then she jumped onto
the big broad nose of the
Oldest-of-All-Crocodiles.
He was the last
crocodile in the line.

"Twelve crocodiles,"
called Small Deer.
"Twelve crocodiles in all!"

With that, Small Deer jumped
to the field of green reeds
on the other side of the river.
She looked back at the crocodiles.

"Thank you, crocodiles," she said.
"Thank you for helping me
across the river."

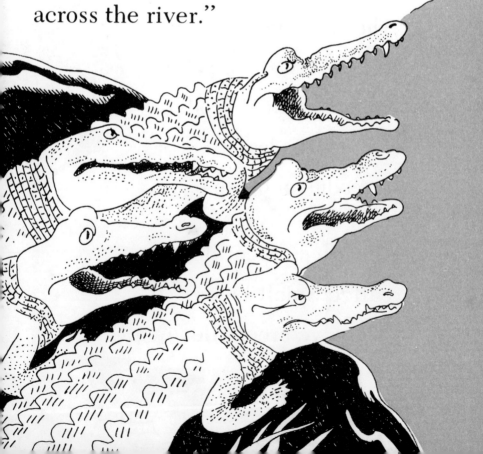

Then all the crocodiles
began to roar and shout.
"War on Small Deer!"
roared the Oldest-of-All-Crocodiles.
"Yes! War on Small Deer!"
"War on Small Deer!"
shouted all the crocodiles together.

But Small Deer didn't hear them.
She was busy playing leapfrog
in the field of green reeds.

## Small Deer's Magic Leaf

One morning,
Small Deer was chasing shadows
when—ker-plop!—
she fell into a deep, dark hole.

The walls were too steep
and the walls were too high
for Small Deer to jump out.
So she sat down to think.

Soon Pig came by.

He looked into the dark hole
and laughed.

"Silly Small Deer," he called.

"Why are you sitting
way down there?"

Small Deer picked up a big leaf.
She began to move her eyes,
this way, that way,
as if she were reading the leaf.
She said to Pig,
"I am reading this Magic Leaf."

"What does it say?" asked Pig.

"The Magic Leaf words say
that the world will end today,"
answered Small Deer.
"Only those
in the Deep Hole
will be saved."

Pig shouted,
"Then I will come down
into the Deep Hole with you!"

"No, no!" said Small Deer.
"You sneeze too much, Pig!
For it is written here that
anyone
who sneezes in the Deep Hole
must be thrown out at once."

"I won't sneeze," cried Pig.

"I won't even sniffle, I promise you!"

So saying, Pig jumped,

plip-plop! down into the Dark Hole.

Small Deer

went on reading the Magic Leaf.

Soon Tiger came by.
He looked into
the Deep Hole
and laughed.

"Silly animals," said Tiger.
"Why do you sit way down there?"

Pig called to Tiger,
"Small Deer reads the Magic Leaf.
The words on the Magic Leaf say
that the world will end today.
Only those in the Deep Hole
will be saved."

Tiger roared, "Then I will come
down into the Deep Hole with you!"

"No, no!" shouted Pig.
"You sneeze too much, Tiger!
For it is written that anyone
who sneezes in the Deep Hole
must be thrown out at once!"

"I won't sneeze," cried Tiger.
"Not even one sniff, I promise you!"
So saying, Tiger jumped,
bump-thump!
down into the          Deep Hole.

Then Elephant came by
and looked into the Deep Hole.
"What are you doing down there?"
she asked.

Tiger called to Elephant,
"The words on the Magic Leaf say
that the world will end today.
Only those in the Deep Hole
will be saved."

"Then I will come down there, too!"
trumpeted Elephant.

"No, no!" cried Tiger.
"You are much too big.
And you sneeze too much!
Anyone who sneezes in the Deep Hole
must be thrown out at once!"

"I will not sniff, sniffle,
or sneeze," said Elephant.
"Here I come!"

So saying, Elephant jumped,
crash, bang! into the Deep Hole.

It was very crowded now.
Small Deer went on reading
the Magic Leaf.

Suddenly, Small Deer looked up.
"Pig, are you
going to sneeze?" she asked.

"No, no, not I!" cried Pig.
"See, I will
push my nose into the dirt
so I cannot sneeze!"

Pig pushed his nose into the dirt
and didn't sneeze.
He didn't breathe very well either.

Small Deer went on reading
the Magic Leaf. Then she
looked up again. "Someone
is about to sneeze!" she said.
"Is it you, Tiger ?"

"No, no, not I!" cried Tiger. "See,
I will pinch my nose with my paws
so I cannot sneeze at all."

Tiger pinched his nose with his
paws. He didn't sneeze at all, but
he didn't breathe very well either.

Small Deer looked at the Magic
Leaf, then she looked at Elephant.

"It is you, Elephant," said Small Deer.

"It is you who will sneeze!"

"No, no, not I!" trumpeted Elephant.
"I will sit on my trunk
and never sneeze one sneeze!"

Elephant sat on her trunk
and never sneezed even one sneeze.
But she could hardly breathe at all.

Suddenly,

Small Deer dropped the leaf.

Her nose went up

and her sides went out.

"AHHHHH . . ." went Small Deer.

"Don't sneeze, Small Deer!"
shouted Pig.
And Elephant and
Tiger shouted, "Stop! Stop!"

But Small Deer did not stop.
She rolled her eyes
and opened her mouth.

"AHHHHH . . .
KERRR . . .

CHOOOOO!" went Small Deer.
Then, with one terrible voice,
Elephant, Tiger and Pig
shouted, all together,

"Small Deer has sneezed!
She must be thrown
out of the Deep Hole at once!"

Then the animals
took hold of Small Deer
and threw her high up

and out of the Hole.

Small Deer looked down at
Pig, Elephant and Tiger.
"Thank you, my friends," she said.

Then, trippity-trip,
Small Deer trotted off to find lunch.
But Pig, Tiger and Elephant
sat in the Deep Hole all day
waiting for the world to end.

Betty Boegehold is an author who particularly delights in writing for beginning readers. Her Pippa Mouse books—*Pippa Mouse* and *Here's Pippa Again*—have brought pleasure to thousands of young readers, as have *Three to Get Ready, Paw-Paw's Run,* and *What the Wind Told.*

A Phi Betta Kappa graduate of Wellesley and holder of an MA in education from Columbia Teacher's College, Ms. Boegehold has worked as a classroom teacher, remedial reading teacher, librarian, and assistant principal. She once ran her own nursery school.

Now a senior associate editor at Bank Street College in New York City, and a children's literature instructor at the school's graduate division, the author is also a New York representative of the Society of Children's Book Writers and a judge on the panel for the Golden Kite Award.

Jacqueline Chwast's lively drawings have added zest and charm to over 25 children's books. Her zany portrait of tantrum-throwing Dover Beech in Beverly Keller's *Don't Throw Another One, Dover!* and *Small Deer's Magic Tricks* join the growing list of such creations as *I Like Old Clothes, Picnics and Parades, Sing Song Scuppernong,* and *Aunt Bella's Umbrella.*

The artist is also a master at creating magnificently detailed paper cutouts, in addition to being a contributor to such magazines as *Harper's, New York, Ms.,* and *Scholastic.*

She and her two daughters, Eve and Pamela, are currently living in New York City.